# The Passover Parrot

This
**PJ BOOK**
belongs to

_____

_____

**PJ Library®**
JEWISH BEDTIME STORIES and SONGS

**Evelyn Zusman**
Illustrations by **Kyrsten Brooker**

**KAR-BEN**
PUBLISHING

## The Story of Passover

The first Passover happened long ago in the far-away country of Egypt. A mean and powerful king, called Pharaoh, ruled Egypt. Worried that the Jewish people would one day fight against him, Pharaoh decided that these people must become his slaves. As slaves, the Jewish people worked very hard. Every day, from morning until night, they hammered, dug, and carried heavy bricks. They built palaces and cities and worked without rest. The Jewish people hated being slaves. They cried and asked God for help. God chose a man named Moses to lead the Jewish people. Moses went to Pharaoh and said, "God is not happy with the way you treat the Jewish people. He wants you to let the Jewish people leave Egypt and go into the desert, where they will be free." But Pharaoh stamped his foot and shouted, "No, I will never let the Jewish people go!" Moses warned, "If you do not listen to God, many terrible things, called plagues, will come to your land." But Pharaoh would not listen, and so the plagues arrived. First, the water turned to blood. Next, frogs and, later, wild animals ran in and out of homes. Balls of hail fell from the sky and bugs, called locusts, ate all of the Egyptians' food.

Each time a new plague began, Pharaoh would cry, "Moses, I'll let the Jewish people go. Just stop this horrible plague!" Yet no sooner would God take away the plague than Pharaoh would shout: "No, I've changed my mind. The Jews must stay!" So God sent more plagues. Finally, as the tenth plague arrived, Pharaoh ordered the Jews to leave Egypt.

Fearful that Pharaoh might again change his mind, the Jewish people packed quickly. They had no time to prepare food and no time to allow their dough to rise into puffy bread. They had only enough time to make a flat, cracker-like bread called matzah. They hastily tied the matzah to their backs and ran from their homes.

The people had not travelled far before Pharaoh commanded his army to chase after them and bring them back to Egypt. The Jews dashed forward, but stopped when they reached a large sea. The sea was too big to swim across. Frightened that Pharaoh's men would soon reach them, the people prayed to God, and a miracle occurred. The sea opened up. Two walls of water stood in front of them and a dry, sandy path stretched between the walls. The Jews ran across. Just as they reached the other side, the walls of water fell and the path disappeared. The sea now separated the Jews from the land of Egypt. They were free!

Each year at Passover, we eat special foods, sing songs, tell stories, and participate in a seder—a special meal designed to help us remember this miraculous journey from slavery to freedom.

KAR-BEN PUBLISHING, INC.
A division of Lerner Publishing Group, Inc.
241 First Avenue North
Minneapolis, MN 55401 USA
1-800-4-KARBEN
Website address: www.karben.com

PJ Library Edition ISBN 978-1-5124-2885-8

Manufactured in Hong Kong
1-41566-23391-9/1/2017

031824.8K1/B1184/A6

I loved our brownstone house in Brooklyn. It had a large, homey kitchen and lots of room upstairs. Best of all was the big backyard with the tall oak tree that shaded us from the summer sun. My brothers Joey and Saul and I loved to play there, especially in the springtime.

One day our neighbor, Mrs. Brown, knocked on our door.

"Good morning," Mama said. "What's that you're holding? Your parrot!"

"Yes, Mrs. Cohen. I'm moving. Wouldn't you like to keep him?" She noticed me, tugging at Mama's skirt, and pushed the cage into my hand. "For you, Lily, a present."

And before Mama could say, "Seven children and a parrot!"
Mrs. Brown was gone.

I jumped with such delight that I scared the parrot
half to death. Mama shook her head. "More
things to take care of," she grumbled.

"I'll help you, Mama. You'll see."

It was shortly before Passover, and Mama was cleaning the house, removing all the hametz, the leavened foods we can't eat on the holiday. She began to refer to the parrot as "that hametzdikeh bird," and before long, we all called him "Hametz."

"Can you say the Four Questions in Hebrew?" Papa asked me a few days before the seder.

His smile seemed to say, "It's okay if you can't." But Joey was old enough to ask them in English, so I made up my mind to learn them in Hebrew.

"Mama, will you listen to me say the Four Questions?" I asked. But Mama was too busy. "Ask Joey to listen to you."

I asked Joey.

"Why me?" he said. "Ask Saul or Rachel or Franny."

"Never mind," I replied.

In the end I chose Hametz. He was never too busy to listen. In fact he loved it when I practiced.

"Mah nishtanah halailah hazeh . . ."

I sang. And Hametz repeated in his parrot-squeaky voice:

"Mah nishtanah halailah hazeh . . ."

**"Mi kol halaylot,"** I continued.

"Mi kol halaylot," squeaked the parrot.

Would Papa be surprised!
I could hardly wait for the seder.

At last the day came. David and Franny helped Mama
in the kitchen. Rachel and Saul set the table. Joey, Becky,
and I checked that everything was in order.

"Haggadot?" Joey asked.

"Check," I said.

"Charoset?"

"Mmm!" Becky said, sampling some.

"Wine?"

"Enough for every cup and Elijah's, too," Papa called from the kitchen.

The guests arrived all dressed up. After we admired
the table, we took our places, and Papa began the seder.

He broke the middle matzah and put half back under the satin cover. He wrapped the other half in a napkin.

"This is the afikomen," he said, putting it behind the pillow on his chair. "Whoever brings it to me after dinner will get a reward."

We all smiled.
Joey laughed. He had already taken the afikomen.
"Here, Lily. Hide it quickly," he whispered.

I snatched the napkin with the afikomen and ran upstairs to my bedroom. As I slipped back into my seat, Papa called, "Quiet, everyone. Lily will ask the Four Questions."

I stood on a chair and began to sing:
**"Mah nishtanah halailah hazeh . . ."**
And as I paused to take a breath, Hametz, who had been sitting quietly in his cage in the living room, repeated in his squeaky parrot voice:

**"Mah nishtanah halailah hazeh . . ."**

All eyes turned to Hametz. I tried to continue.

**"Mi kol halaylot."**

The parrot squeaked right after me, **"Mi kol halaylot."** My brothers giggled. The guests laughed, too.

"Take the parrot up to the bedroom," Papa ordered.

"Mi kol halaylot."

When I came back I sang the Four Questions without a single mistake. The guests clapped, and Papa smiled.

With the sweet singing and the delicious meal, I forgot about the parrot.

At last, Papa called for the afikomen so we could finish the Seder.

"Joey, do you have it?"
"No, Papa."
"Saul, do you have it?"
"No, Papa."
"Lily?"
"Yes, Papa."
"May I have the afikomen please?"

I ran to my bedroom, but there was no afikomen.
I looked under the table and under the bed.
No afikomen. And there was no parrot, either.
The cage door was wide open and Hametz was gone.

I sat down on the floor and began to cry.
Papa sent Joey, and he searched, too. Then
came Saul. In a minute, he knew exactly
what had happened.

"Follow me," he said.

Joey and I followed him down the stairs, through the kitchen, and out the back door into the yard.

There was Hametz, perched on a branch of our tall oak tree, holding the afikomen tightly in his beak.

"Somebody has to climb the tree," Saul said.
"You'd better go," said Joey. "I might tear my new pants."

"No, don't go," I said. "Just let me talk to Hametz."
Then, at the top of my lungs, I sang as loudly as I could,

Hametz couldn't resist. He opened his beak and repeated, **"Mah nishtanah . . ."** The afikomen dropped.

Did Joey catch it? Did Saul?

No! I caught it myself! Well, what was left of it. When I turned around, the whole family and all our guests were standing behind me, watching and clapping.

As we returned to the house to finish the seder, we heard echoes of a squeaky voice singing, **"Mah nishtanah . . ."** Hametz had flown quietly back through the window into the cage. Perched on one leg, he was practicing for the second night's seder.